Don't tell lies, Lucy!

A cautionary tale

Phil Roxbee Cox

Illustrated by Jan McCafferty

Edited by Jenny Tyler
Designed by Non Figg

This is Lucy.

Lucy often tells lies.

Once, Lucy tore her T-shirt.

4

"I was kidnapped by pirates!" she cried.

"Don't tell lies, Lucy!"

Lucy's mother sadly sighed.

Once, Lucy broke a window.

Once, Lucy made a big 'SPLASH!'

Once, Lucy did some drawing
on her bedroom wall.

"It wasn't me," said Lucy.
"A famous artist came to stay."

"Don't tell lies,
Lucy!"
...said her Auntie May.

Lucy's borrowed Paul's bike.

She rides into a tree.

"It wasn't my fault, Paul.
A bandit jumped in front of me!"

Paul runs off angrily to find their family.

"There'll be no more lying, Lucy!

We can't take it anymore!"

"But I'm *not* lying," Lucy lies.
She stomps her foot upon the floor.

She runs from room...

to room...

to room...

slamming every door.

While Lucy's sulking on her bed

and told she must behave...

...heading for their house, is a
GREAT BIG WAVE!

"Everybody out!"
shouts Dad.

"A HUGE WAVE
is on the way."

The others hurry through the door...

...but Lucy's going to stay.

"You are lying, Dad," she shouts.

"I don't believe a word you say!"

Which is how the
GREAT BIG WAVE COMES...

...to wash Lucy far away.